16-10.07

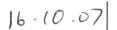

For Rachel Trease

Text copyright © 1997 Geoffrey Trease
Illustrations copyright © 1997 Pauline Hazelwood

This edition first published in Great Britain in 1997
by Macdonald Young Books, an imprint of Wayland
Publishers Ltd

Macdonald Young Books
61 Western Road
Hove
East Sussex
BN3 1JD

Find Wayland on the internet at http://www.wayland.co.uk

Typeset in 16/24 Meridien by Roger Kohn Designs
Printed and bound in Belgium by Proost N. V.

British Library Cataloguing in Publications Data available

ISBN 0 7500 2190 X
ISBN 0 7500 2191 8

Geoffrey Trease

Elizabeth,
Princess in Peril

Illustrated by Pauline Hazelwood

MACDONALD YOUNG BOOKS

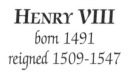

HENRY VIII
born 1491
reigned 1509-1547

married:

1. CATHERINE OF ARAGON (divorced 1533)
   2. ANNE BOLEYN (beheaded 1536)
      3. JANE SEYMOUR (died 1537)
         4. ANNE OF CLEVES (divorced 1540)
            5. CATHERINE HOWARD (beheaded 1542)
               6. CATHERINE PARR (survived him)

MARY I	**ELIZABETH I**	**EDWARD VI**
born 1516	born 1533	born 1537
reigned 1553-1558	reigned 1558-1603	reigned 1547-1553

1
A Royal Appointment

"What chance for poor Elizabeth?"
I could hear my parents talking in low
voices behind the yew-hedge. Father
sounded worried.

They had been pleased when an
important gentleman like Sir William
Cecil chose me to work for him. Now, he
wanted to lend me to the young princess.

One of Sir William's duties
concerned the estate of old Hatfield
Palace where she had been sent back to
live. It would save him much riding to
and fro if he had me there on the spot.

In Elizabeth's household! Almost a
royal appointment. Surely, I thought,
my parents would be delighted. Clearly
they were not. They saw me now –
I was hesitating so as not to interrupt
them. They called me softly. I joined
them. Still keeping their voices down,
for fear of servants, they explained.

"There could be danger," said Father,
"working for Her Royal Highness."

My people are not grand, but they are proud of their long-standing links with the House of Tudor. Grandfather was one of the group of boys picked to share lessons with the future King Henry the Eighth. They became friends. Years later, when Henry was king and marrying his third wife, Jane Seymour, he asked Grandfather to send his son, *my* father, as page to the new queen.

Father came to know both of Henry's daughters by his previous wives – Mary (who by now was our queen) and her little half-sister Elizabeth. Both their mothers were dead.

That was when my parents first met. My mother, Ursula, was a maid of honour to Queen Jane, so she too had known the lively three-year-old redhead, Elizabeth. I had expected her to be delighted now at the news that I, a generation later, was to follow our family's tradition of royal service. Now, I learnt why there was a problem that worried her.

It all went back – as most things seemed to in those troubled days – to religion. In particular to Henry the Eighth's quarrel with the Pope in Rome, who would not agree to the divorce the King wanted.

Mary's mother, the divorced Queen Catherine of Aragon, remained a devout Catholic and brought up Mary the same. The next queen, Anne Boleyn, was not, or she would not of course have felt free to marry the divorced King. She was a Protestant, and so was Elizabeth.

By this time the English people were getting divided into Catholics and Protestants, mostly Protestants – like my father's family and my mother's. *They* thought King Henry was head of the Church in England, but the Catholics said the Pope was.

My parents had only a year together in Queen Jane's household. The poor woman died after giving birth to the little son the King so badly wanted. So Queen Jane's court was all broken up. My father and mother might never have met again. Luckily they did, a few years later, or there would have been no me.

All this was now ancient history, but I had picked it up in odd scraps when my parents and my grandfather discussed old times. That afternoon in the garden I saw more clearly how the facts fitted together and might affect my own future.

King Henry the Eighth died when Jane's son was barely ten, but he at once took the throne as King Edward the Sixth. He had a strong group of noblemen to guide him, and they were all Protestants, so it seemed as though the new form of religion was firmly established. But Edward spoilt everything because he was delicate and died before he was sixteen – younger than I was myself at that moment.

Princess Mary became Queen. There was an armed revolt. She wanted to bring back the old Catholic faith. Most people did not. Mary won. She gave her half-sister a spell in prison in the Tower as a warning to keep out of the dispute.

Then Mary married Philip of Spain. If they had a son he would inherit the throne after her. There would be no risk of Elizabeth becoming a Protestant queen.

"They've had no child," said Father.
"They won't now. But I don't fancy
Elizabeth's chances of ever being queen.
She's almost a prisoner even at Hatfield.
Well-treated – but one false move and
she'll be back in the Tower. Maybe her
head cut off, as her mother's was."

"So don't *you* get mixed up in
anything, Guy," my mother pleaded.

2
Almost a Prisoner

Hatfield was not the gloomy place I had feared. It was a quadrangle of russet brick, with clustered lime trees, fine gardens, and a park dotted with great oaks. Once a bishop's palace, it had been taken over by King Henry the Eighth as a quiet home, far from court, for his orphan children.

Elizabeth had spent much time there since she was little. It had happy memories, it did not feel like a prison. The gentleman in charge there, Sir Thomas Pope, was kindly and treated her with respect. She had her own ladies-in-waiting to attend her. She could do as she liked.

Except *go*.

She was twenty-three now. Quite
tall, with that red-gold hair and striking
eyes. Dignified, but full of life, ready for
music or a dance or a ride.

She showed me the quiet room where she would dictate her letters and issue instructions. I found her kind and friendly. "You will treat everything as confidential, Master Guy."

"Of course, Your Royal Highness."

"Sir William Cecil trusts you absolutely. *I* trust *him*."

Some private letters she wrote herself, in a beautiful hand. Though she was so lively she loved to study. She knew French and Italian, Latin and Greek, even some Spanish and German, She said, with a laugh, "Thank God, if I were turned out of England in my petticoat I could live anywhere!"

Sometimes I was invited to join her in a day's hunting. We made quite a cavalcade with her twelve ladies in white satin and twenty yeomen in green, the Tudor colours. The country folk welcomed her so warmly. She had always a smile and a word.

Once, when we were out hunting, a gaunt old shepherd pulled off his cap and knelt in the road and waved a book at her.

"God bless Your Royal Highness!" He poured out a torrent of words like a preacher. He begged her to defend the Protestant religion. She gave him a kindly answer but her ladies looked scared.

He was a well-known local man who denounced the old Catholic worship Queen Mary was bringing back. Elizabeth might agree with what he was saying but she had better not show it.

Weeks later I saw why. That shepherd, John Hyson, had been arrested as a herctic, an unbeliever. He might be burned at the stake.

In London alone seventy-four people had met this horrible end. It was this bitter argument over religion. I saw now why my parents (though they were Protestants like Elizabeth) were uneasy about my working in her household.

3
A Dangerous Letter

Mostly the princess took her exercise
in the park. She liked, with my help, to
plant young oak saplings. Some days
that autumn were mild enough to sit
and read. It was easier to talk freely.
People could not listen behind curtains.

Once the princess sent me to fetch her book. The usual serving-maid was tidying the study. She was facing the window, waving a sheet of paper in front of her. I startled her. She spun round. Her hands flew to her throat.

I murmured something to reassure
her. I was searching for the book.
Glancing down, I had a feeling that the
princess's own papers had been disturbed
in their drawer.

I saw something else. A spot of ink,
shining black and wet on the desk-top,
newly spilt.

Who had just been writing? Not Sarah. She could not read or write. I think that was why the princess had chosen her to do this room, so that she would not pry.

I tried to sound casual. "Any one been in here?"

"No, sir." She sounded worried.

"It *is* true? You cannot read or write?"

"Sir, I'm just an ignorant country girl."

I saw the corner of white paper below her throat. Tucked into her high bodice, not quite out of sight. "Then what's that paper?"

She scowled down, flushed, and shoved it further. "Nothing, sir."

"Show me." I put out my hand.

"For shame, sir!" She was older than I thought. Harder. But I must guard those private papers.

"Let me see what you are hiding." The paper had popped back into view.

She blazed like a wildcat. Her knee shot up. There was a hefty leg under that homespun skirt. My padded trunk hose were not padded enough. I yelled and let go.

She dashed out of the room. I went after her. If she got rid of that paper I should have no evidence.

She raced across the deserted gardens, between the clipped shrubs, making for the little gate in the brick wall. Once through there she could hide the paper and collect it later.

I was gaining on her. She reached
the gate – it was like a wooden door –
she yanked it and shot through into the
quiet lane beyond. I was too close for
her to shut it behind her.

I heard thundering hoofs. A
horseman galloped to meet her. She
held out the folded paper.

He was still too far away. I grabbed
her hair and jerked her backwards. She
tumbled over with a screech. I snatched
the paper.

"Catch him!" she gasped. "Get it back –
if you have to kill him ..." But I was back
in the gardens, running. Halfway to the
house I glanced round. The man had not
followed. Nor had the girl. No one at
Hatfield ever saw her again.

Clearly a spy. Not for Queen Mary,
I think. More likely for her Spanish
husband, Philip, or for the extreme
English Catholics who were so strongly
against Elizabeth.

She *could* write though, this Sarah. In a hasty scrawl she had copied some letter that had been sent to the princess by a gentleman offering his services, with a band of armed men, *'in this present danger hanging over you.'*

I stopped there. I was not meant to read this. I must take it to the princess at once. I remembered the book she wanted, fetched it, and ran all the way to where I had left her.

"You have been an age," she said severely. Then, seeing my face, she added, "What has happened, Guy?"

"I met Sarah. She had just been copying this from one of your private papers."
I handed her the paper with a bow.

She frowned at the untidy writing. "You have read this?"

"Only enough, Your Royal Highness. When I saw how secret it was – "

"You will keep it to yourself," she said swiftly. "With her majesty in her present poor health it could make trouble. If I accepted this gentleman's kind offer I might seem to be plotting against her. Who knows where that might lead?"

She knew, and so did I, Elizabeth had enemies who could use such a letter to send her to her doom.

"As you have read this much," she said with a smile, "I will tell you what I have answered. I thanked him – but said no." She sighed. "I must take my chance."

4
What Chance for Elizabeth?

Often in life Elizabeth was to take
chances. She was no coward. I remember,
thirty years later, her wonderful speech
to her troops at Tilbury, mustered ready
to drive back the Spanish troops if they
tried to land from the ships of Philip's
Armada.

She had been warned, she told them, not to risk herself *'in armed multitudes, for fear of treachery'*. "Let tyrants fear!" she cried. "I am come among you resolved in the heat of the battle to live or die amongst you all, to lay down for my God, and for my kingdom, and for my people, my honour and my blood, even in the dust." I never forgot those words. But she never took chances unless it was necessary.

In that anxious autumn of 1558, at Hatfield, she knew that her father had meant her to be queen if both Edward and Mary died without children. But King Henry had not foreseen how sharply divided England would have become between Catholics and Protestants, each side desperate to choose the next ruler.

Mary was determined to bring back
the old faith. She had tried hard to
convert her sister. Elizabeth was tactful.
She considered Mary's arguments. But
it was not yet the law of the land that
everyone must be a Catholic. If it ever
was, she would of course obey. Mary
had to make do with that.

The half-sisters had not met for nine months. Mary was not fit to travel. She did not ask Elizabeth to visit her and Elizabeth could not leave Hatfield without permission. What would happen if Mary died? We all wondered. The princess gave us no hint.

Rumours reached us from court. Mary's health got worse. She was only forty-two, but some whispered she could not last long.

Her husband was far away in Europe.
Philip had no real love for her. He had
married her hoping she would have a
son who would inherit her kingdom and
keep it in the Catholic faith. He knew
now that she would never bear a child.
He had lost interest in her – but not in
the throne of England.

Somehow he would hold on to
England. He would back some other
claim against Elizabeth, make sure she
could not take the crown.

No wonder that maid had been planted at Hatfield. There might be other spies. And probably men in the palace to stop Elizabeth if she made a bolt for it. Only in the great park could she stroll at will.

Father's words kept coming back to me. What chance for Elizabeth? I wondered constantly. I think she did too. Would there be some dreadful act against her? Something we could not foresee?

5
The Day of the Horsemen

I shall never forget the day the horsemen came. It was a mild November afternoon. We were sitting underneath one of those old oak trees she loved.

The riders had seen us. They broke into a canter, heading our way. What a lot of them there were! What chance should we have if –

I jumped to my feet. Was this an arrest? I stood, heart in mouth. The princess had not moved an inch. Her eyes were fixed on the horsemen.

They reined in. They swung from their saddles. They swept off their hats. They actually knelt on the grass. Their leader began: "Your majesty –"

Majesty? Could I believe my ears?

"We, the Lords of the Council, have come to inform you –"

Queen Mary had died that morning.
Elizabeth had instantly been proclaimed
queen. Parliament, being mainly Protestant,
meant to block any other claim at the start.

Now Elizabeth herself fell on her knees.
She exclaimed, "It is the Lord's doing, and
marvellous in our eyes."

I was kept busy that day. Elizabeth's first thought was to send for Sir William Cecil. He was the one man in the world she thoroughly trusted – and how right she was! She at once made him her Secretary of State. I sat with them, pen in hand, making notes as they directed. They had to word her first public proclamation.

They had several tricky points to discuss. Her list of official titles, for instance. King Henry the Eighth had called himself 'Supreme Head of the Church'. So had her brother Edward. But Mary, as a devout Catholic, would not claim the title for herself. Should Elizabeth please the Protestants and take it back?

They talked anxiously. Use it or not? Whatever she did, one section of her subjects would be offended. What would they decide, she and Sir William? Suddenly she turned and smiled at me. "I know," she said. "Simply write *'etcetera'.*"

Just like Elizabeth! That was often how she was to govern England over the next forty-five years.

5359

PRINTED IN BELGIUM BY

proost

INTERNATIONAL BOOK PRODUCTION